URKEL...AFRAID OF THE SCHOOL BULLY???

Steve pulled off his mitten. "Sir, I will have you know that it is people such as yourself who put the 'ick' in 'pathetic.' Not only have you harassed and insulted me, but you have sullied the reputation of my lady love...."

Before Willie could figure out what all those big words meant, Steve slapped him clean across the face with his mitten.

Willie was too amazed to do much of anything at first. Then he started to sputter. "He...hit me...with his mitten!" he said to Waldo, and to anyone else who would listen. A crowd had gathered, hoping for a fight.

Waldo nodded. "Be careful. He's got another one."

Willie grabbed Urkel's mittens and pulled them out by the elastic bands. Then he snapped them back hard.

"Urkel, you are dead meat!"

Family Matters™
The Lean, Mean Urkel Machine

by Bonnie Worth

Based on the series FAMILY MATTERS™, *created by*
William Bickley & Michael Warren

and developed by
Thomas L. Miller & Robert L. Boyett

and on episodes written by
David W. Duclon
Dennis Snee & Fred Fox, Jr.

A PARACHUTE PRESS BOOK

Parachute Press, Inc.
156 Fifth Avenue
New York, NY 10010

ISBN: 0-938753-61-4
Printed in the United States of America
February 1992
10 9 8 7 6 5 4 3 2

The Lean, Mean Urkel Machine

One

IT WAS A TYPICAL evening at the Winslow house, nestled in a peaceful neighborhood in a suburb of Chicago.

Carl, the head of the household, had not come home from work yet. He was a policeman for the Chicago metropolitan police force—and proud of it.

Eddie, Carl's fifteen-year-old son, was in the kitchen, about to leave for basketball practice. But before he left, he just had to taste one of his grandmother's freshly baked Mississippi mud cookies. Mississippi mud cookies were Carl's mother's specialty. Eddie took a cookie right off the baking sheet.

"Yeow!" he cried out.

"The ones on the plate are cooler, Edward," his

mother said from behind the evening paper. She was sitting at the kitchen table watching her son.

But Eddie was in a hurry. "Gotta go," he said, blowing on the hot cookie. He popped it whole into his mouth before stepping into the living room.

Harriette Winslow smiled to herself and shook her head. *That boy sure does love his cookies*, she thought. *Takes after his father that way.* She returned to the paper.

Mother Winslow slipped the last batch of cookies into the oven. Then she turned to her ten-year-old granddaughter, Judy, who had been helping her.

"Now, Judy, tell Grandma, what was the secret ingredient? Can you remember?"

"Of course I can." Judy giggled as she licked the delicious, chocolaty mixing bowl. "It's mud!"

Judy's four-year-old cousin Richie had claimed the big wooden spoon for himself. Richie and his mother, Rachel, lived there, too. Rachel, Harriette's "baby" sister, and Richie had moved in after Rachel's divorce.

Little Richie was licking the wooden spoon like it was a huge chocolate lollipop. "Yummy mud!" he said.

"It's not *really* mud," Judy explained to her little cousin. "It's chocolate. But the secret ingredient," she said to her grandmother, "is orange peels. See, I remember!" she said proudly.

"I'll make a baker out of you yet!" her grandmother said.

"Hmm—MMM." Harriette put down the newspaper, leaned back, and breathed deeply. "Every time you bake these, they smell better and better."

"Why, thank you." Mother Winslow smiled at her daughter-in-law. "I promised Carl if he stuck to his new diet for a month, I'd reward him with a plate of his favorite cookies."

Harriette laughed. "Some diet!"

Meanwhile, out in the living room, Laura, Harriette and Carl's thirteen-year-old daughter, was sitting on the couch painting her nails. She, too, smelled the delicious aroma as it wafted in from the kitchen. *Dad must be on a diet again*, she thought. Her grandmother always baked Mississippi mud cookies when Dad went on a diet. Kind of weird, if you asked her—but nobody had asked her. She couldn't complain, though, because Mississippi mud cookies were her favorite, too.

"Ding-dong, Urkel calling!"

Laura paused halfway through painting her longest fingernail and rolled her eyes toward the ceiling.

Nobody else in the world had such a high, pinched, nasal voice. And it was much too loud. At times Urkel's voice sounded like a cross between a smoke alarm and a sick cow.

When Laura didn't say "Come in," Steve Urkel poked his head around the door. "Oh, good! You're home!" he said.

Nobody else looked like Steve Urkel. He had goggle eyes, a crew cut, and horn-rimmed glasses with a black elastic strap to hold them around his neck.

Examining her nail-polish job, Laura sighed. "Come in," she said, sounding bored. "Since I guess you're already in," she added. She wasn't exactly overflowing with enthusiasm at the sight of him.

On the other hand, the sight of *her* couldn't have pleased Steve more. "Good fortune smiles upon me!" he declared.

One of the first things people noticed about Steve were his long legs, which had grown much faster than the rest of him. They made him look more like

4

an eight-year-old walking around on stilts than the fourteen-year-old that he was.

And it was certainly true that nobody—but nobody—would dream of dressing like Steve Urkel. He wore clunky saddle shoes, white socks, a varsity sweater, and gray dress pants with red suspenders that hitched them up, as always, almost to his armpits.

Steve was the Winslow family's nearest neighbor. The son of a busy brain surgeon and his equally busy wife, Steve spent more time at the Winslow house than he did at his own. He had the annoying habit of dropping in any time, day or night. And when he did, he always had an opinion to offer, whether anybody asked for it or not. For instance:

"That nail polish is the perfect shade for you, my dear," he said.

"Thanks, Steve," Laura said dryly.

Yes, he was Steve Urkel: Wiz Kid, child prodigy, class-A nerd. And every once in a while, Laura didn't like to admit, he was a good friend.

But tonight... well, tonight, she just wasn't in a Steve Urkel kind of mood. She was, if the truth be told, in a Greg Hudson kind of mood. Greg Hudson was the best-looking boy in school.

"Here it is Friday night and a delightful creature such as yourself is actually at home!" Steve said.

Laura finished applying polish to her pinkie fingernail and blew on it. "I'm home," she told him. "But don't get your hopes up. If Greg Hudson finishes studying for his algebra test, I'm outta here. He said he'd take me to see the new *Halloween Street* movie."

"*Part IV?*" Steve shuddered. "I avoid horror movies myself. They horrify me beyond my capacity to cope."

Laura stared at him. She didn't see why Steve had to speak like he was a walking college dictionary.

He translated for her benefit: "What I mean is, horror movies scare the living daylights out of me."

Laura smiled knowingly. "Me, too. But not with Greg Hudson by my side."

Steve let loose with one of his usual snorts. "The very idea of your placing yourself at the beck and call of that…that—"

"Hunk?" Laura finished for him. She screwed on the lid of the nail-polish bottle.

"What's he got that I haven't got?" Steve whined.

Everybody knew that Steve Urkel's crush on Laura Winslow was harder to kill than the zombie maniac in *Halloween Street*, parts I through IV.

"What's he got that you haven't got?" Laura answered. "Try looks, for starters."

Steve scoffed.

"Money," Laura threw in.

Steve thought about that.

"And how about a personality that doesn't drive me clear up the wall and down the other side?" she added for good measure.

Steve nodded his head firmly. His eyeglasses caught the light and flashed. "Very well put, my dear. But I can dream, can't I?" He gave her a puppyish look.

Not as far as I'm concerned, she thought.

Just then, Laura's aunt Rachel bounded down the stairs. She held out a pair of long, heavy gold bangle earrings.

"Hi, handsome!" Rachel said to Steve, who was now lounging on the couch, making himself at home. Rachel sidestepped his long legs to get to Laura.

For some bizarre reason, grown-ups—the female

kind in particular—seemed to like Steve. Laura couldn't figure out why. Maybe it was because he was sort of an old-fashioned goody-goody.

"These are the earrings I was telling you about," Rachel said to her niece. "They'll go great with your new green sweater, don't you think?"

"They're gorgeous!" Laura said, taking the earrings. She was lucky to have a young, cool aunt living under the same roof with her. It was almost like having a big sister. Especially when it came to borrowing things. "And you'll really let me wear them?"

"For a date with Mr. All-Right, you've got to look Dyn-o-mite," Rachel said, grinning. "Besides, now that you've got your ears pierced, I've got lots of earrings you can borrow. But don't you go and lose these now or I'll be all over you like a bad case of German measles."

"Don't worry, I won't," Laura assured her aunt. The earrings really were pretty.

Steve, who made Winslow business his business, peered critically at the earrings in question.

"Losing those would be like losing the Washington Monument in a haystack," he pronounced.

"Are you sure you want to burden your delicate lobes with those wrecking balls?"

Laura ignored Steve. Just like she did most of the time. "Can I try them on?" she asked her aunt.

"Of course." Rachel led Laura over to the nearest mirror. "The wires are pretty thick, so go easy threading them through your earlobes."

Steve crept over and watched. He made a face. "Why you women feel obliged to punch holes in your ears in the name of beauty truly mystifies me," he said.

"Ouch!" Laura winced. "They're kind of hard to get in. I guess my holes aren't completely healed up yet. The lady who pierced them said sometimes it takes a little time for them to toughen up."

Rachel nodded. "She was right about that. See? You're bleeding a little."

"Blood!" Steve shrieked.

Laura and Rachel heard a crash. They turned from the mirror and blinked in surprise. Steve had keeled over in a dead faint.

"Gee," Rachel declared, "for a surgeon's son, that boy is mighty squeamish."

Two

LAURA AND RACHEL knelt over Steve and fanned him with a magazine until he came to and sat up.

"Oh…oh! Ladies, forgive me. I must have tripped on something and fallen. How very clumsy of me."

"Tripped!" Laura sputtered. "My foot! You didn't trip. You fainted. And this isn't the first time."

Steve struggled to his feet. Brushing off his varsity sweater, he tried to look dignified.

"You ladies are mistaken. Steve Urkel never faints. And now…if you'll excuse me, I have urgent business on the home front."

Laura and Rachel watched him make his exit on rubbery legs. He looked pretty shaken up. Just as the door closed behind him, Harriette burst in from the kitchen.

"What fell?" she exclaimed. She looked ready for disaster.

Laura laughed. "Nothing much. Just Steve."

Harriette looked around. "Is the boy all right? Was he hurt?"

Laura shook her head, amazed at how much concern her mother showed for Urkel. Sometimes, it seemed as if she thought of him as her second son.

"He wasn't hurt," Laura told her mother. "He just fainted. He was watching me try on Aunt Rachel's earrings. By accident, I pricked my ear and I guess one look at one teeny-weeny drop of blood was too much for him. He passed out cold. What a world-class sissy!"

Rachel shook her head. She didn't like it when people insulted Steve. It wasn't his fault he was so strange—or was it?

Laura's grandmother joined them in the living room. She was carrying a pot of tea, cups, and a plate of Mississippi mud cookies, steaming from the oven. Richie and Judy came in after her, each holding a cookie on a napkin.

Mother Winslow set the tray down on the coffee table. "What's all this hissy about sissies?" she demanded to know.

"We were talking about Steve Urkel," Laura said. She helped herself to a cookie and filled her grandmother in on the earring episode. "I mean, we are talking Gutless Wonder here," she finished.

Rachel and Harriette chuckled. Though they were both fond of Steve, they had to agree with Laura. Steve Urkel wasn't like any other person in this world.

Mother Winslow clucked her tongue in disapproval. "How quickly we all forget," she said as she began to pour the tea.

"What do you mean?" Harriette asked her mother-in-law.

"I am merely remembering a time not so very long ago, Harriette, when that *Gutless Wonder* was willing to defend your daughter's honor. When no one else—including Mister 'Moneybags' Hudson —had the pluck to do so."

Harriette and Rachel looked a little ashamed.

Nodding, the sisters took their cups of tea and settled down on the couch. Mother Winslow did have a point.

But Laura didn't have the slightest idea what her grandmother was talking about. All she knew was that "pluck" wasn't exactly the word that came to mind when she thought about Steve Urkel. She stirred sugar and milk into her tea.

"Don't you remember how bravely he came to your defense?" Laura's mother prodded her.

"To my *what*?" Laura shook her head. "When did he ever do that?"

"Why, that boy was willing to risk his neck for you," Mother Winslow said.

"His neck!" Laura exclaimed. Were these women crazy? "I don't know what you're talking about."

"I guess you need a little reminding then," Mother Winslow said. "Although I am frankly surprised. I mean, it was only a year or so ago. Spring, I think it was."

Suddenly, Laura knew what they were talking about. "You mean the Sadie Hawkins Day Dance?"

The three older women nodded solemnly.

Over tea and cookies, all four of them remembered back to that evening, a year ago last spring, when the subject of the Sadie Hawkins Day Dance first came up.

Three

IT HAD BEEN a school night. Laura had just come downstairs to get herself a study snack. She was wearing a purple bathrobe over her nightgown. Getting a snack was really just an excuse—an excuse to bring up the dreaded subject of the Sadie Hawkins Day Dance to her mother. She had a feeling her mom would give her a hard time.

"Night, Mom," Laura said, passing through the living room on her way back upstairs from the kitchen. In one hand she carried a plate of grapes; in the other a notebook.

"Night, honey," Harriette said absently. She was busy opening the day's mail. *Too many bills*, she thought, shaking her head.

"Have a grape." Laura popped a grape into her mother's mouth. "Anything interesting?"

"If you call the bills for cable TV, electricity, the phone, the oil, three credit cards, and the mortgage interesting," Harriette said, "then I'm truly fascinated."

"Well! I guess I'd better go study." Laura headed for the stairs. Then she paused. *Now,* she told herself, *now is the time to do it.* "After all, the school dance is next week." She tossed the words ever so casually over her shoulder, and waited—one second, two seconds—for the bomb to go off.

"Whoa, whoa, whoa!" her mother exploded. "School dance? What's this about a school dance?"

Laura turned. Her smile was angelic. "You know, Mother dear," she said in her sweetest voice. "It's the Sadie Hawkins Day Dance. Girls ask boys. I'm gonna ask Greg Hudson."

Harriette raised a suspicious eyebrow. "Have I met him?"

Laura leaned wistfully against the railing. "No, but picture a Greek god...with his own moped."

"Well," her mother said, "just make sure Mr. Apollo has you home before eleven."

"Eleven?" Laura echoed in outrage. "When are

16

you gonna realize I'm becoming a mature woman?" She tossed her sleek black pageboy in defiance.

"When you can get through breakfast without spitting Cheerios at your sister," Harriette returned smartly.

Laura couldn't argue with her there.

"Hey," Harriette went on, "is that the new nightgown I bought you?"

"Yeah."

"Let me see you model it."

Reluctantly, Laura laid down the grapes and notebook. She shrugged off her robe and modeled the new nightgown dutifully. She had asked for hot pink baby-doll pajamas, but her mother had said no way and picked out the same old boring granny gown.

"Very pretty," Harriette approved.

Laura groaned aloud.

Just then, the front door opened. In walked Steve Urkel—without knocking, as always.

"Hello, gang!" he twanged. At the sight of Laura, he pulled up short. "Oh! Laura! Nightgown!" was all he managed to get out before he fainted.

Disgusted, Laura put her robe back on.

"Are you okay?" Harriette asked Steve.

"I'm fine," he stammered, recovering. "I guess it was just the shock of seeing Laura in her unmentionables. Ooops!" He clapped a hand over his mouth. "I mentioned them!"

"Mom!" Judy called from upstairs. "Richie keeps trying to eat the pieces of my pepperoni-pizza jig-saw puzzle!"

Harriette put down the phone bill with a sigh. "Duty calls," she said. She went upstairs to rescue Judy's puzzle from little Cousin Richie.

Laura glared at her mother. Deserter! How could she go off and leave Laura alone with the world's biggest pest. "What do you want, Steve?" She picked up her books and snack and headed toward the stairs.

But Steve went after her and, taking her arm, dragged her toward the couch. "Only to serve you, milady. Let me relieve you of your burdens." He took the snack and notebook from her, led her over to the couch, and sat her down. Then, to the tune of "Camptown Races," he sang: "Let's sit you down upon the couch, doo-dah, doo-dah. Gonna pop some grapes into your mouth, Oh the dooh-dah day.

18

"Now you're in your place, I can fan your face...."

Laura grabbed back the notebook he was fanning her with. "Steve," she said through clenched teeth. "*Exactly what do you want?*"

"Oh." Steve undertook a serious study of the ceiling. "I just thought you might like to ask me to the Sadie Hawkins Day Dance." He batted his eyelashes at her.

Laura took back her plate of grapes less violently than she had the notebook. "Uh, Steve, listen." He might be a nerd, but even nerds had feelings. Particularly when the nerd had a crush on you that would not quit.

"I was going to wait for you to call," Steve went on. "Then I realized it would be like waiting for your brother, Eddie, to be invited to come on *Jeopardy*." Laugh. Laugh. Snort.

Laura's big brother, Eddie, was a nice boy but he wasn't exactly known for his brains.

Laura gathered her courage. "I was gonna ask Greg Hudson to the dance," she said.

Steve was shocked. "Greg Hudson?"

Laura nodded.

"The smart, good-looking, rich guy?"

Laura nodded.

"But why?" Steve's whine was even more irritating than usual.

"Well, 'cause I sorta like him a little," she confessed. "Actually, a lot...actually, a whole lot."

Steve bit his lip. He turned away quickly. "I see. I see. Uh..." For once, he was at a loss for words. Then he found some.

"I really hope you and Greg have a good time. You'll probably get stuck going in a limo...which is too bad, because my cousin was gonna take us in his horse trailer...."

Laura avoided looking at Steve's face, but he sounded strange. "Are you all right?" she asked gently. That was the way it was with him. One minute he was bugging her, the next minute, making her feel sorry for him.

"Yeah. I'm all right," he told her. "It's...it's just something in my eye. That's all." He took off his glasses and wiped his eye on his sleeve.

Then he turned to Laura and put on a brave smile. "Well, what do you know? It was my very own finger!"

"Steve, I didn't mean to hurt you. I just don't want to lead you on."

Steve squared his shoulders. "I know. I'll tell you what. You go ahead and ask Greg 'Teeth-Are-a-Little-Crooked' Hudson to the dance. But if he turns you down—a decision which could only be the result of brain damage—I'll be there waiting with the ol' horse trailer. Deal?" He stuck out his hand.

Laura smiled and shook it. Steve really did have his charming moments. Even if there was only about one a decade!

"Deal," she told him.

Four

AT SCHOOL the next afternoon, Willie Fuffner, the school bully, was up to his usual nasty tricks. He strolled along, passing lockers on both sides of the hall, until he reached Steve Urkel's locker. There he came to a dead stop.

"Hey, watcha gonna do, Willie?" his not-too-bright sidekick Waldo wondered dully. Waldo was an all-around yes-man.

Willie just grinned in an evil sort of way. "I'm gonna trash Urkel's locker," he said.

Waldo blinked. "Why you gonna do that, Willie?"

"'Cause it's Tuesday," Willie answered.

Waldo blinked. "Again?"

Willie took a huge screwdriver out of his pocket and began to pry open Urkel's locker.

The second it opened, a siren went off. It echoed up and down the hall, louder than a car alarm in a parking garage. Some kids just getting out of class stared at Willie.

Quickly, Willie put the screwdriver into Waldo's hand. He then went over to his own locker. Trying to look busy and innocent, he began to work the combination. It was obvious that he had no idea what the numbers were. And looking innocent was one thing Willie Fuffner just couldn't do.

Meanwhile, as soon as the alarm had gone off, Steve Urkel came running down the hall as fast as he could. He could have moved faster if he hadn't been carrying half a dozen extremely heavy textbooks.

He set the books down. Then he reached into the locker and expertly deactivated the alarm. Silence at last!

Then he looked around for the culprit. He didn't have to look far, since Willie's locker was only a few lockers away from his own.

Steve walked right up to Willie and tapped him on the shoulder.

"All right, come clean, Fuffner. I know you're the guilty party," Steve challenged him fearlessly.

Willie turned around and grinned. "Not me, Potato Face."

"Potato Face?" Urkel repeated thoughtfully. "Brilliant use of the English language."

He turned and addressed the crowd of students that had gathered to watch.

"Fellow students, I beg of you. Isn't there one of you with the guts to come forth and testify against this brute?"

No one said a word. The students just stood there staring up at Willie. Without blinking, Willie returned their gazes. Suddenly, everybody seemed to have to get to classes on the other side of the building. It was common knowledge that Willie Fuffner was the toughest kid in school. Satisfied with himself, Willie headed over to the drinking fountain.

Seeing the scattering students made Steve shake his head in disgust. "Sheep! You're all sheep," he said. He returned to his locker and inspected it for damage. Just some bent metal around the lock, which could be easily fixed. Fortunately, the rest of the locker was in perfect shape. It was a good thing too, for Steve Urkel's locker was no mere locker.

Not only was it the single neatest locker in the entire school. It was the most organized and the best-furnished one, too. He had designed it to suit his special needs. It had built-in bookshelves and a pegboard to hold his school supplies. On the back of the door, he had even hung an 8″x10″ glossy photograph of his lady love, Laura Winslow. His locker was a regular home away from home.

He was staring at the photograph of Laura in adoration when the real Laura Winslow came walking down the hall. Laura stopped at her locker, swiveled the dial on her combination lock, and opened it.

Steve recognized the sound of her locker door— a much sweeter sound than the other locker doors— and turned around.

"Hi, Laura," he called over to her. He then turned back to the photograph and blew a secret kiss to her image.

But Laura had scarcely heard his greeting. She was too busy looking past him—at Greg Hudson, who had just arrived at his own locker only a few feet away. She gathered up some courage and approached him.

"Oh, Greg?" she said shyly. Up close, he looked even more handsome than usual. Asking him out wasn't going to be easy. What if he said no?

"Hi, Laura," he answered.

"Hi," she said.

"Hi," he said.

"Enough of this small talk," she blurted out. "Would you like to go with me to the Sadie Hawkins Day Dance?"

Greg smiled. He seemed about to say yes. Then he caught sight of Willie, who was pulling posters off the bulletin board. Greg's smile faded.

"I...I can't Laura," he stammered. "I mean, I'd like to, but—"

"You don't have to explain." She backed away. Her cheeks were burning. How humiliating! "I understand," she said stiffly.

She turned and walked back to her locker. Like a robot, she removed her coat, got her books, slammed her locker shut, and walked down the hall with what was left of her dignity. Never, ever again would she invite any boy anywhere!

"No!" Greg called after her lamely. "You don't understand."

Steve, who had been putting on his coat, had witnessed the entire drama. He had seen it but he didn't believe it!

He adjusted the clips on his mittens and attached a mitten to each coat sleeve. Then he put on his mittens and stepped boldly up to Greg.

"Good grief, man! Have you just taken leave of your senses? You were just asked out by the most wonderful woman in the world."

Greg leaned closer. "Would you keep your voice down?" he whispered. "Believe me, I'd like to go with Laura, but Willie won't let me."

Steve's eyes narrowed. "Fuffner? The Locker Looter?"

Greg nodded solemnly. "Fuffner told Laura he wanted her to ask him to the dance. She said no and that Sadie Hawkins Day meant *lady's* choice and her choice was *not* Willie."

"That's my spirited spitfire!" Steve said proudly.

Greg gave Steve a strange look. Why in the world did he talk like that? "Yeah, well," said Greg, "Willie's getting back at her. He put out the word that any guy who goes to the dance with Laura will end up breathing through his ears."

"Ah!" Steve stroked his chin. "So he wants her to go to the dance alone?"

"Worse," Greg answered. "He wants her to go with *you*."

Steve was outraged. "Why, the swine!" He wanted to go to the dance with Laura, but not like this.

He knew only one thing: Willie Fuffner was terrorizing his true love, and that meant war!

He unzipped his coat, which was a struggle since he was wearing his clip-on mittens. Then he strode over to Willie. There was only one way to solve a dispute like this: man to man.

Steve lifted his hand and prepared to tap Willie on the shoulder. From close-up, that shoulder looked large and extremely muscular. For a split second, it occurred to Steve that challenging Willie Fuffner was perhaps not a very wise thing to do. He would probably get pounded. But that would be a small

28

price to pay for Laura's honor. He took a deep breath and tapped Willie on the shoulder with all his might.

Willie whirled around, fists raised, ready to fight. But when he saw it was Steve, he just laughed. Waldo, who'd been standing on the sidelines, laughed when he saw Willie laugh.

"If it isn't Mighty Mouse!" Willie jeered.

"I have heard some low things in my time," Steve said. "But forcing Laura to go to the dance with me...well, that's just plain despicable."

Willie took it as a compliment. "Thank you," he said.

Steve pulled off his mitten. "Sir, I will have you know that it is people such as yourself who put the 'ick' in pathetic. Not only have you harassed and insulted me, but you have sullied the reputation of my lady love...."

Before Willie could figure out what all those big words meant, Steve slapped him clean across the face with his mitten.

Willie was too amazed to do much of anything at first. Then he started to sputter. "He...he hit me...with his mitten!" he said to Waldo, and to anyone else who would listen. A crowd had gathered, hoping for a fight.

Waldo nodded. "Be careful. He's got another one."

Willie grabbed Urkel's mittens and pulled them out by the elastic bands. Then he snapped them back hard.

"Urkel, you are dead meat!"

"And you," Steve returned calmly, "are brain dead."

It took two guys to hold Willie back and keep him from punching Steve.

Steve hid behind the two tallest eleventh-graders he could find. As he crouched down low, he held up his fists. "Hold me back! Hold me back!" he cried, punching air.

Other kids were urging the boys on. "Fight, fight, fight!" they chanted.

Coach Redding heard the ruckus from down the hall in his office and came to break it up. He held Willie by the scruff of his neck in one hand; Steve in the other.

"You two wanna take a little trip to the principal's office?" he asked.

"No, sir!" Steve declared. Going to the principal's office would damage his record as an honor student. Besides, the principal scared the living daylights out of him. "I only wish to give this philistine the punishment he so richly deserves," he said.

Willie sputtered some more. "What did he call me?"

Waldo shrugged. "Phyllis somebody, it sounded like to me."

Willie struggled to free himself from the coach's grip. "Nobody calls me Phyllis and lives to tell."

"Let him go," Steve said to the coach, knowing full well the coach would do no such thing. "He's mine!"

"So I take it this is a fight you both want to finish?" Coach Redding asked.

Willie nodded firmly; Steve less firmly.

"Yeah," said Willie.

Steve pointed at Willie. "I want you. I want you. I want you."

"Noon, Saturday, Silver's Gym. In the ring with proper supervision," the coach told them. Then he released them both.

"I'll be there, Coach," Willie said. "But I got ten bucks says Urkel won't even show."

"Oh, I'll be there, all right, Fuffner," Steve assured him. He gathered up his load of books, shut his locker, and headed down the hall. "I'll be there with bells on," he called over his shoulder.

Waldo turned to Willie and looked puzzled. "You really think he'll wear bells?"

Five

THE NEXT AFTERNOON, Laura's father, Carl, took Steve to the boxing gym for a little prefight instruction.

Coaching Steve Urkel on his day off was not Carl's idea of a good time. Carl and Steve had a sort of love-hate relationship—Carl loved to hate Steve. But when Laura looked at Carl with those big brown eyes and begged him to help, how could he say no? He'd probably live to regret it, but he just couldn't let his older daughter down.

Carl knew a little something about boxing. After all, he was a cop and a cop had to know how to handle himself in a fight. He had done some boxing in the army, too. "Carl the Crusher," they had called him. Those were the days!

Carl believed anyone could defend himself if properly coached. Well, maybe *almost* anyone, he thought when he looked at Urkel. Today, Steve wore a pair of baggy sweatpants held up, practically to his chin, by red suspenders that matched his brand-new boxing gloves.

The gym was noisy and crowded with guys grunting, sparring, pounding bags, and pumping iron. It smelled of sweat, gym shoes, and leather.

And then there was Steve Urkel, who fit in about as well as a ballerina in a ballpark.

"Gee, Carl," Steve shouted over the noise, "thanks for helping me hone my skills!" He began prancing about, boxing with an invisible opponent. Shadowboxing, the pros called it.

"I'm so fast, I'm so pretty...I'm a lean, mean Urkel machine." Steve was even trying to talk like a pro, cocky and ready to take on the world.

With his arms folded across his chest, Carl watched Steve. "Are you sure you wanna go through with this?" he asked. Steve's pipe-cleaner legs and coat-hanger shoulders showed him to be one sorry excuse for a fighter.

"I have to. Laura's honor has been impugned by

that pugnacious pile of putrid pond puke."

Carl sighed heavily. Half the time, he didn't even understand what the kid was talking about. Urkel used bigger words than the average certified genius. "If you boxed half as well as you shot your mouth off..." he began. But he knew it was no use. "All right. Climb into the ring. Let's see how much you have to learn."

Steve started to climb over the ropes, but he got tangled and fell nose-first onto the mat. *Oof! Splat!* Unfazed, he picked himself up. "Ready," he said.

Carl shook his head sadly. "Okay, show me your fighting stance."

Steve spread his long legs wide apart and held up both gloves in front of his face as if he were hiding.

"How's this?" he asked. His nasal voice was muffled by the gloves.

"Great," Carl said, "if you're fighting the Easter Bunny. All right now, show me your fighting style."

Steve sprang into action, waving his arms crazily about.

"Steve," Carl said patiently.

Steve kept at it, punching the air wildly.

"Steve!" Carl said, a little less patiently.

Steve kept flailing away.

"STEVE!" Carl bellowed.

Steve stopped. "Hmmmm?" he asked innocently.

"That's not a fighting style," Carl informed him tartly. "That's a plea for help."

"Teach me, Carl."

"All right, I'll try. But Steve, I strongly suggest that you consider a different strategy. Instead of trying to hit your opponent, try *running* from him."

Steve nodded cannily. "Ah...sort of like an Urkel Shuffle?"

"Exactly."

"I'll work on my Shuffle, but could you show me a few punches?"

"Okay," Carl said reluctantly. "Assume the fighting stance."

They faced off in the ring, like opponents. Urkel was gloved; Carl was barefisted.

"Now, Steve," Carl began. "A boxer's most important punch is the jab. The jab is a quick, straight blow to your opponent's face. Now, let's see your jab—"

Steve's glove flicked out, catching Carl square in the nose.

"How's that?" Steve asked innocently.

Carl scowled and rubbed his nose. "Fine, fine. Just next time, wait till I'm ready."

"Ooooh. Sorry, Big Guy," Steve said.

"Now, another good punch is the left hook. The arm travels in a circular motion, connecting with your opponent's chin."

Carl demonstrated, stopping short of hitting Steve's chin. Steve nodded. This was easy!

"And it's a real good punch to have," Carl continued. "Especially if the other guy's just using his jab...."

At the word "jab," Steve jabbed. Again, Carl got it right in the nose.

Carl grabbed his nose. It was beginning to feel sore.

"Sorry," Steve apologized once more. "Just reflex."

Reflex, your mama, Carl thought. But he just glared and continued the lesson.

"Another good punch to have is the right cross. It's a power move—a knock-you-out punch. Now, when you see an opening, your right hand comes across your left hand with all your weight behind it. Like this...." Again, Carl demonstrated. Again, he stopped short of actually connecting with Steve's face.

"Now, you don't want to overuse your right cross," Carl said. "You want to save that for the perfect moment. Most of the time, you'll be relying on your left hook and your jab—"

Out came Steve's glove with a jab. Carl got it in the face.

Rage welled up in Carl. He counted to ten before speaking. "That's enough for today, Steve," he said as sweetly as he could. Carl turned away to rub his poor nose. He didn't want Steve to know just how much it hurt.

Then again, maybe this was a good sign. *Maybe there's hope for Steve after all,* he thought. *If Willie Fuffner lets his guard down the way I have today.... Who knows? Maybe the Lean, Mean Urkel Machine really will come through in the pinch. Stranger things have happened.... Whoa there, Carl, stop kidding yourself.*

Six

SATURDAY ARRIVED all too soon. And along with it a larger than average crowd at the doors of Silver's Gym. They were there to see the celebrated bout: Urkel versus Fuffner.

The entire Winslow family had come to watch. Mother Winslow led the way, carrying her knitting bag. "Because I'd just as soon not watch," she said.

Rachel was there, with little Richie, who was wearing a pair of kid-sized boxing gloves. "I want to be just like Steve," he said.

"I don't think that's such a good idea," said Eddie, "considering the odds against him." Some of Eddie's high school friends had shown up, just for the fun of watching Fuffner pound Urkel into the mat like a tent peg.

Laura held tight to her mother's hand. Being afraid for Steve had given her a bad case of the jitters.

"Don't you worry," Harriette told her daughter. "Everything's going to be fine." Then she added, under her breath, to her sister, "I only wish I believed that."

"I know what you mean," Rachel murmured, eyeing the empty ring. "It all looks so...official."

Since the Winslow family had arrived early, they got the best seats in the bleachers. Carl had come even earlier to help Steve warm up. Naturally, he was going to serve as Steve's corner man during the fight.

Lots of kids from school had come, too—including Greg Hudson. He couldn't resist saying hi to Laura as he passed her in the bleachers. Laura returned his greeting sullenly.

"You okay?" Greg asked.

"No, I'm not," she burst out. "It really bugs me that Steve is the only guy with enough guts to stand up to Willie."

Embarrassed, Greg hung his head and slunk off to find a seat. Just then, the locker-room door banged open and Willie Fuffner pranced out. The crowd gasped. Willie looked frightening in his boxing trunks and headgear. Everyone felt sorry for Steve.

Willie raised his gloves over his head in a champion's salute to the crowd. They responded with boos, hisses, and jeers. Willie thumbed his nose at them.

Then Steve came out. The words "Iron Man Urkel" were stitched on the back of his flashy green robe in bright red letters. He turned around to receive the crowd's applause.

Carl held the ropes so Steve could climb into the ring. Steve, trying to look cool, nodded his thanks to Carl. But then...*boing!*...*smash!* He dived nose-first onto the mat—just as he had at practice. People laughed, thinking this was part of the show.

With as much dignity as possible, he picked himself up off the mat, rubbed his nose, and went to his corner. There he removed his robe, revealing trunks that were pulled up to his armpits—in the usual Urkel fashion. A few people in the crowd snickered unkindly.

Steve took off his glasses. Carl handed him a

rubber mouthpiece to protect his teeth from Willie's punches. Steve tried not to think about Willie's punches. He repeated the words "Lean, Mean Urkel Machine" over and over to himself.

Meanwhile, up in the stands, Mother Winslow nudged Rachel, who sat next to her. "Steve sure looked like a real pro in the robe we made him," she said.

Rachel nodded. "He was really touched when I gave it to him." Then she added with a grin, "He wants to be buried in it after the fight."

Mother Winslow frowned. She didn't see what was so funny. That foolish, brave little boy had gotten himself into a heap of trouble this time. But there was no time to fret. The first round was about to start.

Coach Redding stepped into the ring, and the buzzing crowd quieted down.

"Ladies and gentlemen," he addressed them. "What we have here is a three-round grudge match. In this corner, weighing in at one hundred and forty-two pounds, 'Hurricane' Willie Fuffner."

The boos were thunderous. Willie stood up, and Waldo removed his footstool.

"And in this corner," the coach said over the boos, "at ninety-seven pounds soaking wet, Steve 'Iron Man' Urkel!"

The crowd cheered wildly. Carl removed Steve's footstool, but Steve was too involved with the crowd to notice. He backed up to sit down, but— *splat!*—he landed sprawled on the mat. Laughter mixed with the cheers. Hastily, Steve got to his feet and brushed off the seat of his trunks.

Coach Redding frowned at all the nonsense. Boxing was serious business.

"All right, gentlemen," he said solemnly. "You hear the bell, you come to the center of the ring, you touch gloves, you begin fighting. You got that?"

Willie and Steve nodded.

Bong.

Willie strolled toward the center of the ring. Steve rushed at him. Willie held up his gloves for the touch. Steve crashed into them and fell to the mat.

Up in the stands, Mother Winslow commented to Rachel, "He lasted longer than I thought."

The coach stood over Steve and began the count: "One...two..."

Steve shook his head, then jumped to his feet.

The coach said, "Start fighting!"

Willie came at Steve punching. Steve ducked.

"Steve! Steve!" Carl called out. He waved his hands. He stomped on the mat. He tried everything short of standing on his head and whistling "Dixie" to get Steve's attention.

"Not now, Carl," Steve told him, as he ducked punches. "I'm a little busy."

"Remember the Urkel Shuffle," Carl urged him. "Stay away!"

Now Steve remembered! Instantly, he pranced out of Willie's range, using his fanciest footwork.

Willie had to run to keep up as Steve danced away from him. First clockwise, then counterclockwise, Steve moved in neat circles. For the longest time, Willie couldn't get close enough to land a single punch on his opponent. Steve grinned.

Willie was beginning to look tired. Steve was feeling good. He was even feeling cocky enough to wave to Laura in the bleachers. This was kind of fun!

Then Willie caught on to Steve's strategy. As Steve completed one of his circles, Willie was waiting for him with a cocked fist. *Womp... crunch...boom!* Steve sank into the mat.

"One...two...three...four..." Coach Redding stood over him, counting.

Once more, Steve managed to come to his senses and get to his feet. Only this time, his legs were a little rubbery. He went for the safety of his corner.

Frantically, Carl waved him back toward Willie. "Keep fighting, son. The round's not over yet!"

Steve nodded wearily and turned back toward the center of the ring. "Shuffle!" Carl called out to him. But every time Steve tried his Shuffle, he wobbled and sank to his knees.

"I can't!" he called back pitifully. "He broke my Shuffle."

"Steve," Carl said, "I think we should throw in the towel."

"No way!" Steve squeaked. "If I can just hit him once, with all my might, I'll drop him like a bad habit."

Just then Fuffner sneaked up on him. "Come on, fight," he sneered.

Steve turned and Willie hit him hard on the chin. Steve's eyes crossed and he went down again.

"One...two...three...four...five..." As Coach Redding counted, Steve struggled to rise. At six, he made it to his feet. Again, he staggered toward the ropes.

Laura couldn't stand it another minute. She jumped up from the bleachers and ran to the ringside.

"Laura?" Steve peered out at her blearily. "Why, there's three of you. Oh, the world doesn't deserve such riches!" he croaked blissfully.

"Steve," Laura begged, practically in tears. This was all her fault. "Stop getting back up," she said. "Just stay down."

But Steve wasn't going to do that because this wasn't about giving up. This was about fighting for a principle. For honor. For the love of Laura. "Don't worry, my little kumquat."

Steve lunged away from the ropes to where Willie was waiting for him. Actually, there seemed to be four Willies. And all four of them punched Steve—hard. He crumpled to the mat.

Again, Coach Redding began the count.

46

"One...two...three..."

"Steve, stay down," Carl told him.

"...four...five..."

"Steve, please stay down," Laura pleaded.

"What did you say?" Steve asked.

"Stay down," she said.

"What did you say?" Steve repeated.

Everyone in the bleachers shouted together, "SHE SAID 'STAY DOWN'!"

But Steve just couldn't do that. With a mighty heave, Iron Man got to his feet just before the coach got to ten. He swayed against the ropes. Iron Man? He was more like Jello Man at this point.

"All right, Fuffner!" he called out, fearless as ever. "Quit stalling. Where are you, huh? Now take that...and a little of that...." Like a drowning man, he flailed about, punching thin air. Everybody in the gym was positive he was about to go down for the last time.

Willie pranced over and got ready to deliver the knockout punch. Suddenly, someone in the bleachers shouted, "Hold it!" All eyes turned to Greg Hudson.

"Hey, Willie!" Greg said. "I'm tired of you

pushing us around. If Urkel can stand up to you, so can I. So after you finish him, you're going to have to fight me!"

"*After?*" Steve said weakly. He was feeling quite finished already, thank you very much.

Another boy stood up. "And then me," he said.

Still another stood up. "And me."

But Willie wasn't scared. "Come on!" he sneered. "I can take you all on!"

Just then, more boys rose to their feet, too. Fists clenched, they expressed their willingness to take on the bully.

Willie counted heads. He would have to fight more than a dozen guys. And there were probably more waiting in line. There was no way he could handle those odds.

Waldo spoke up. "Uh, what you gonna do now, Willie?"

It didn't take Willie more than a quarter of a second to reach a decision. "Run!" he replied.

And run he did. Out of the ring and straight toward the locker room.

Waldo looked around. His eyes widened as he saw dozens and dozens of unfriendly faces. "Me,

48

too, Willie!" he cried. "Wait up!" And Waldo, too, ran away.

"Ladies and gentlemen," Coach Redding declared, "the fight's over!"

On cue, Steve keeled over onto the mat. Carl, who had been standing off to the side, came over and pulled Steve to his feet. He sponged off Steve's face with cold water.

Laura climbed into the ring. "Steve, are you okay?" she asked tenderly.

"I seem to be all right," Steve muttered vaguely.

Carl unlaced Steve's gloves and pulled them off. Steve stared at his bare hands.

"I don't seem to be seeing things or experiencing any other signs of concussion."

Laura grinned. "That's my Steve, the doctor's son."

Greg joined them. "Hey, Laura, if you still want me to go to the dance with you, I'd like to."

"Thanks, Greg," Laura told him. "But I've decided to go with my champion." She turned back to Steve. "Steve, will you go to the Sadie Hawkins Day Dance with me?"

Steve's head reeled. He held it in both hands.

"Oh, no! I was wrong. I may not be seeing things, but I sure am hearing them!" Everybody laughed.

Carl held up Steve's limp arm. "Ladies and gentlemen, the winner by a principle—Steve Urkel!" The crowd roared its approval.

Seven

MOTHER WINSLOW shook her head fondly. "I can still hear that crowd in Silver's Gym. How they cheered for our boy! They sure knew a champion when they saw one."

She got up and went into the kitchen to refill the empty cookie plate. She knew Carl would be coming through the door any minute now. After a day on police duty, he'd be hungry for some predinner cookies.

Mother Winslow knew her son, all right. Right on cue, the front door opened. Carl was home. Richie pedaled past him on his tricycle and waved. "Hi, Uncle Carl."

Judy looked up from her workbook. While the grown-ups had been telling the Urkel story, she had been practicing her math. "Hi, Daddy," she chirped. "I learned how to add all these numbers together!"

"Good for you, sweetheart," Carl told his younger daughter.

Carl set down his duffel bag and waved to the group over on the couch. "Good evening, ladies." He took off his black bomber jacket, which he wore over his policeman's uniform. Then he paused and sniffed the air like a bloodhound. "Could it be?"

"It most certainly could," his mother said, coming out of the kitchen. At the sight of the plate of cookies she held, Carl rubbed his hands together. Mississippi mud cookies!

"Hello, Mississippi!"

His mother smiled and poured him a cup of tea. "Care to guzzle tea as you wallow in the mud?"

Carl looked hurt. "I hope I wasn't interrupting your dainty little tea party."

"Hardly," said Laura. "Actually, we were talking about Urkel."

Carl stiffened. "Are you trying to ruin my appetite?" He picked up his cup and three cookies.

"I think I'll just take my snack and leave you ladies to your idea of fun."

"Oh, you're fond of Steve and you know it," Harriette teased him.

"He's the second son you never had," Laura added.

"The second son I'm *glad* I never had," Carl corrected his daughter.

"Actually," Harriette put in, "we were just remembering the time you coached Steve for that fight in Silver's Gym."

"The things I've done for that boy. And the things he's done *to* me!" Carl rubbed his nose at the memory of Steve's practice punches.

Rachel said, "We were saying that Steve, for all his nerdy, obnoxious ways, is actually kind of a brave little guy."

"They convinced *me* of it," Laura said cheerfully. "And it wasn't easy."

Carl made a face. "Well, nobody's gonna convince me." Honestly. This was really too much for him. "You're calling Steve Urkel brave? *Brave!*" Here he was going out on the streets every day, risking his neck to fight crime and put bread on the Winslow table. And here the women were sitting around praising not him, Carl Winslow, public servant and model husband and father, but Steve Urkel, neighborhood pest!

"Why, that little pantywaist wouldn't last a day on the street—"

"Pantywaist, is it now!" Mother Winslow cut her son off cold. "Who are you calling pantywaist? Aren't you the one who used to get the swirly-swirlies every time you climbed up a stepladder to change a lightbulb?"

Instantly, Carl looked sheepish. "Well, I did suffer from a fear of heights at one time. But not anymore."

"And who was it who cured you of that fear?" his mother pressed him.

Carl hated to admit it, but there was really no denying it. "That little pantywaist next door," he said. And, in spite of himself, he smiled at the memory. When had it been? A year ago last summer. He had been a different man then, and in many ways, a lesser one.

It had been a work night, just like this one. His

shirt, as he walked in the door from work, had stuck to him. Only it hadn't been the heat that had made him sweat. It had been fear....

Eight

HARRIETTE HAD BEEN sitting on the couch, catching up on some office paperwork, when Carl came home from work that August night. One look at her husband's face and Harriette knew there was something wrong.

"What is it, dear?" she asked.

Carl didn't answer. Instead, he simply drop-kicked his duffel bag across the room.

"Carl!" she cried out, truly concerned now. This wasn't the big teddy bear she had married.

"What?" he growled.

"Why are you so upset?" she asked.

He sighed and shook his head. But then he confessed. "I was chasing this young punk across the roof of the Sears Tower," he began.

The Sears Tower was a steel and glass skyscraper that loomed above the Chicago skyline. It was the tallest office building not only in Chicago, but in the entire world. The Sears Tower was so tall that in high winds, it actually moved. Like a giant tree in a gale, it swayed back and forth, ever so slightly.

Carl went on with his tale. "This punk had been snatching purses and, as I was chasing him, I happened to glance over the eh-eh-eh-dge...and I fro— fro—"

"Froze?" she finished for him.

Carl touched his nose. "You got it. I mean, I started shaking and sweating. I got dizzy. I have not felt that sick since the day I met Steve."

"Well, did you catch the guy?" Harriette wanted to know.

Carl looked glum. "No. He got away when I started to cry. Heights always made me a little nervous, but nothing like this has ever happened before."

"Carl, how did you finally get down?"

"I crawled down the stairs, Harriette, on my hands and knees."

Harriette couldn't believe it. "You mean you

crawled down one hundred and ten flights of stairs?"

Carl rubbed his behind. "Well, actually, I slipped and fell down the last sixty."

"Poor baby!" Harriette said, holding her arms out to her husband.

The day after Carl's humiliating experience on the roof of the Sears Tower building, he was in the living room with Eddie. Eddie was helping him take that first, all-important step toward curing his fear of heights. With a grim, determined expression on his face, Carl stood at the top of a stepladder. It had only three steps, but that was perfect for starters. While Eddie held the ladder steady with his left foot resting on the bottom step, he read a comic book.

"How am I doing, son?" Carl called down, as if from a vast height.

"What?" Eddie looked up from his X-Men comic. "Oh, great, Dad. But how many times are you going to chase a crook up a kitchen ladder?"

"Dr. Van Lowe, our family doctor, says that I should take it one step at a time, gradually building to greater heights."

Eddie nodded and looked back at his comic book. "Makes sense to me," he murmured.

"I want to thank you, son, for helping me out. I really appreciate it."

"Hey, Dad, I'm always here for you."

Just then, the telephone rang.

"That's Jolene!" Eddie cried, dropping his comic book and sprinting off to the kitchen to answer the phone.

"Eddie! Eddie!" Carl called out in vain from the top of the stepladder. So much for Eddie always being there for him.

He looked down. The floor seemed to tilt and swirl, making him dizzier and dizzier. He teetered.

With his back to the door, Carl crouched low and tried to lower himself, one treacherous step at a time.

Just then, with his usual knack for timing, Steve Urkel waltzed in through the front door.

Steve caught sight of Carl. "Hi, Carl!" He waved to Carl's back.

Steve's shrill greeting caught Carl completely off guard, causing him to lean over backwards. Trying to catch Carl, Steve rushed forward—but he was too late. Down came Carl, bringing Steve down with him. Fortunately, the couch broke both their falls.

Carl let his poor shaking bones sink into the cushions of the couch, relieved that he was on safe ground. But something about the cushions of the couch didn't feel right. They felt hard...and knobby. And they seemed to be squirming!

Carl thought he heard an odd, muffled whimpering sound coming from somewhere beneath him. A sound like a helpless Urkel trapped beneath two hundred–plus pounds of heaving Winslow. Realizing now that he had accidentally pinned Steve beneath him, Carl shifted to one side.

"You okay, Steve?" he asked.

Steve lay there for a few seconds in a daze. Then he felt around experimentally. No broken bones. His eyeglasses were intact.

"Okay, I guess," Steve ventured. Then he felt his pocket. "I just wish I hadn't put that darned Ding Dong in my pocket." He pulled out the Ding Dong, smashed flatter than a streamrolled caterpillar.

Carl helped Steve to his feet, flattened Ding Dong and all.

"Steve, what do you want?"

Steve scratched his head. "I don't remember. But I'll tell you what I don't want. No more games of Squish the Urkel."

"Steve," Carl explained patiently. "That's not a game. I'm just working on a little problem I have."

Steve nodded. "Ah, care to fill me in?"

"Not really." Carl busied himself folding up the ladder.

"Oh, come on, Carl," Steve coaxed him. "It's me. You know there's nothing you can't tell me. Share."

Carl shifted, embarrassed. Finally, he said, "Well ... I maybe, sorta have a little problem ... with heights."

Steve nodded in a businesslike way. "Ah, acrophobia, eh? Why don't you learn to conquer your fear. Buck up and go bungy jumping, for instance."

Carl shuddered and sought the safety of the couch. "No way. I get the willies just thinking about heights. No, my doctor recommends that I take it slow."

Steve shrugged. "Okay, if you want to listen to some *medical* guy...."

Before Carl could lose his temper, the doorbell rang. He got up to answer it.

"Lieutenant!" Carl was unable to hide his surprise when he saw his boss, Lieutenant Murtagh, standing on the doorstep. Murtaugh hardly ever came to his house.

"Winslow," said the lieutenant. Then, seeing Steve, he nodded. "Kid."

The lieutenant was a tall, burly fellow. Most of the guys at the station thought of him as a stuck-up fool. For the most part, Carl agreed with that. But Carl was a good cop and always treated his superiors with respect.

"Well, sir, this is a pleasant surprise," Carl lied. "Come in."

As his boss strode in past him, Carl had the sinking feeling this wasn't a social call.

Nine

"THIS ISN'T a social call," Murtagh said gruffly, echoing Carl's thought.

Carl nodded. "I see. Steve?" He pointed to the door. "This is police business."

"Oh, great!" Steve said, failing to take the hint. "I love that stuff."

Carl sighed. *Give me strength*, he silently begged the ceiling.

Murtagh eyed the boy suspiciously. "You look familiar."

"We met once," Steve told him. "You showed me a picture of your dog."

Murtagh nodded. "Right."

"So how is ol' Bloodfang?" Steve asked chattily.

"He's dead."

Steve winced. "Sorry."

"Yeah?" Murtagh sulked like an overgrown six-year-old. "Like that's really going to bring him back." He went over to the couch and sat down.

Steve edged over to Carl and whispered, "They actually give this guy bullets?"

Carl tried to push Steve away as he sat down next to his commanding officer. "So, sir. What brings you to this neck of the woods?"

Steve hung over the back of the couch and, head poked between those of the two men, eavesdropped shamelessly.

"Winslow?" Murtagh grunted. "I've always thought of you as a cop's cop. A top cop. A no-holds-barred nonstop cop."

Carl swelled with pride. "Well, thank you, sir." Steve beamed proudly.

Murtagh continued. "You can imagine my shock when I found out you were a pantywaist."

Steve's jaw fell. So did Carl's. "Excuse me, sir," said Steve. Carl glared at him.

"The hot topic in the officers' steam room is that you're afraid of heights. A real catwalk coward."

Steve pounded the back of the couch with his fist. No one called his big buddy a coward!

"Who?" Carl demanded angrily. "Who says that?"

"I'm not naming names, but it was some of the other patrolmen. I, of course, immediately defended you. I told them no one in my command was a wimp."

Carl looked relieved. "Thank you, sir."

"You can thank me by making an appointment to see the police psychologist."

Steve shook his head sadly. Carl see a shrink? The big guy with a shrunken head? Not a pretty picture. Carl sounded like he was having a pretty hard time with that idea himself.

"Well, uh, sir..." Carl stammered.

Murtagh clapped him so hard on the back he fell forward on the couch and almost choked. "Winslow, I want to level with you. I'm gonna be captain soon. And I'd like to see you make lieutenant and take my place. Now that's not gonna happen if you're up on some roof sweatin' and pukin'."

Carl squared his shoulders. "Sir, you can count on me to take care of my problem."

Satisfied, Murtagh got ready to leave. "That's very reassuring."

Carl smiled widely. Keeping the smile on his face, he walked Murtagh to the door and saw him out. When Carl shut the door, his smile promptly faded.

He began to pace. He began to sweat. Forgetting that Steve was even there, he began to talk to himself.

"Oh, I am in big trouble now. I am in deep Bandini. What am I gonna do?"

But Steve was already working on the problem. He had struck his classic thinking pose—head cocked, chin cradled on fist. He was listening to his thoughts and nodding. Finally, he broke into a wide grin. Yes, he liked what he heard!

"Sir," Steve spoke up at last. "I just received a blinding flash of inspiration."

Carl didn't like the sound of that. Steve's blinding flashes usually started fires. "What?" he asked warily.

"Why, sir, I believe I have a surefire cure for your fear of heights."

Carl shook his head firmly. "I don't want to hear it. I'll just take Lieutenant Murtagh's advice and go see the police psychologist."

"Fine!" Steve told him airily. "You can spend the next five years on the couch whining about your mommy, or you can eliminate your fear of heights in just one day."

Just one day, eh? Carl had to think about that one for a minute.

"One day sounds good," Carl said at last. "Okay, what's your plan?"

Steve walked to the door. "I'll pick you up tomorrow morning at eight. All you have to do is trust me and do exactly as I say."

Carl flinched. Do exactly as Steve said? He pictured himself jumping off the Sears Tower on Steve's say-so.

But it was too late to back out now. He had been foolish enough to place himself in the hands of Steve Urkel. Whatever happened to him now, he probably deserved.

Ten

BRIGHT AND EARLY the next morning, Steve showed up at the Winslows' front door. Carl was ready for him: awake and dressed and, he hoped, prepared for whatever lay ahead.

"Got the car gassed up?" Steve asked cheerfully.

Carl narrowed his eyes. "Yeah," he growled. "So what?"

"We're going for a drive, Big Fella, you and me. Relax and enjoy the ride."

Reluctantly, Carl went outside and got into his car. Steve got into the passenger seat and smiled over at Carl encouragingly. So far so good.

"Don't worry about a thing," Steve told Carl.

"Just follow this handy-dandy map I drew up for you early this morning."

Carl studied the map. The route looked simple enough. "Are you going to tell me where we're going?" he asked.

Steve shook his head. "Sit back and enjoy the pleasant sensation of pins and needles, Carl. You'll find out soon enough."

Carl kept his temper. No sense losing it this early. He had all day for that.

"Whatever you say, Steve." Carl gunned the engine and set off down the road according to the map.

They drove for over an hour until they were well out into the country. It was August, and the fields were a rainbow of wildflowers. Carl was just beginning to enjoy himself when Steve said: "Make a right turn onto this dirt road. We're almost there."

Then Carl remembered this wasn't just a pleasant summer's day outing. Steve had plans for him.

They drove through a field. Up ahead there loomed a large round red and white striped object bigger than the entire Winslow house.

The closer they came, the bigger it looked and the

morc it became obvious that it was one of those hot-air balloons that some maniacs are fool enough to go up in.

"Pull up right next to that hot-air balloon," Steve told him calmly.

Carl slammed on the brakes and turned to Steve. "You mean...?" He couldn't even finish his sentence, but that was okay—Steve finished it for him.

"I'm taking you up in that balloon. Rightaroonie, Big Fella. In my clever, resourceful way, I called up yesterday and reserved us two seats. Fortunately, they were willing to accept my father's credit card. I don't know if my father will accept this—but we'll deal with that later.

Carl looked through the windshield up at the enormous balloon, billowing in the summer breeze. Some cure for his fear of heights! It was kind of like putting somebody with a fear of garden snakes into a pit of deadly black mambas.

Steve got out of the car and came around to Carl's side. He opened the door. "Come on, Carl. Our departure time nears. These tickets aren't cheap, you know."

Carl stumbled out of the car toward the balloon. The closer they got, the bigger the balloon looked. A tiny, run-down shack stood next to the balloon. On the shack door was a sign: WILD BLUE YONDER, INC. Beneath the sign, in smaller lettering, were the words *Fly At Your Own Risk.*

Carl turned around and headed back toward the safety of his car. But Steve wasn't going to let him get away with it. He came after Carl and dragged him back by his sleeve. Carl didn't drag too easily. Fear added to Carl's already hefty weight.

"Carl, you'll be fine," Steve told him.

"Oh, fine!" Carl said nervously. "You expect me to go up in a hot-air balloon?" He didn't even want to look at the thing. Just thinking about himself up in the balloon turned his stomach.

"Listen, Carl," Steve said sternly. "You've got to face your fears and go up in that balloon."

"I do not," Carl said.

"Yes, you do. It's the perfect way to get over your fear of heights. And, remember, if you don't conquer your phobia, you can kiss your badge goodbye."

The kid had a point. Carl turned around and

walked back toward the balloon. This time, he forced himself to examine it. It was huge—maybe four stories high. It was made of some kind of red and white striped parachute silk. The basket people rode in was attached to the balloon by a series of ropes. It looked pathetically flimsy, like an oversized laundry basket. It reminded Carl of Eddie's old backyard treehouse platform. Only, unlike the treehouse, the basket didn't look strong enough to hold his weight, let alone his weight plus that of Urkel and anyone else who might come along.

"Don't these things go really, really high?" Carl asked in a small voice.

"Sure," Steve said. "But we'll try to keep it around five thousand feet."

Carl mouthed the number. Five thousand feet? Why, that was nearly one mile up!

"You can't go much higher than that without oxygen," Steve explained cheerfully. "Otherwise your head will explode."

"Thanks for sharing that with me," Carl said. Then he turned around and headed for his car again. Steve ran after him and tackled him. Usually this wouldn't be possible, but today Carl was so weak with fear that he fell over easily.

The two of them rolled around in the grass until they heard somebody say:

"Okay, gentlemen. We're ready to go."

Carl looked up. A man in a sky-blue jumpsuit was standing over them. He held a coil of rope in one gloved hand.

"Hear that, Carl?" Steve said. "It's lift-off time. What do you say? Anchors aweigh?"

Reluctantly, Carl got up off the ground.

Mr. Sky Blue held out his hand in a friendly fashion.

"Hi, I'm Jimmy 'Wild Blue Yonder' Phillips."

Carl's smile was broad but insincere. "Pleased to meet you. I'm Carl 'Yellowbelly' Winslow."

"You have a fear of heights?" Jimmy asked, interested.

"I do," Carl admitted.

"You're not my first customer with that problem. Let me assure you, hot-air ballooning is a completely safe and risk-free activity."

"Well, that's good to know," Carl said. But he didn't sound very convinced.

"Now, why don't you guys just step up on that little platform there and climb into the basket. Make yourselves comfortable."

Eagerly, Steve hopped into the basket. He had put on a huge, clumsy crash helmet.

Carl pointed to the helmet. "I'm not getting in there if he wears that thing on his head."

Frowning, Steve took off the helmet. "Party pooper. Come on, Big Guy. Come on."

Carl climbed in.

"Good!" Jimmy said. "I'll just get some maps out of the shack. I'll be right back. And then we'll be on our way."

To Carl's alarm, Jimmy disappeared into the shack. Carl waited nervously for their captain to return. Steve passed the time by rummaging around in the bottom of the basket.

Carl drummed his fingers on the side of the basket. Old Jimmy must be having trouble finding his maps. That didn't say much for his navigational skills.

Steve was now examining the rigging. "Gee," he wondered aloud as he fingered the long cord hanging down. "What do you suppose this gizmo does?" He tugged on it. Overhead, a giant flame shot up, making a strange whooshing sound.

The basket rose up off the ground about six inches and hung there, rocking back and forth.

Carl clutched at the sides of the basket. "Steve! Steve! Steve!"

"Oh, the gizmo makes it go up." Steve sounded pleased, having satisfied his scientific curiosity.

"Right," Carl said weakly. "Now make it go down again."

"Okay. Maybe if I pull it again, it'll go down."

Again, he pulled the cord. Again, flames shot up over their heads. There was that nasty whooshing sound, and the basket shot up another foot.

Longingly, Carl stared down at the grass. To think that only moments ago, he had had both feet planted firmly there. Whatever had possessed him to set foot in this basket? He knew what had possessed him—an evil spirit named Urkel.

"Hey, Jimmy!" Carl called out toward the shack. Where was the guy when they needed him? When Jimmy didn't come running out, Carl turned to Steve. "Do something!"

Steve was studying the cord, talking to himself.

"Nope, this seems to be a one-way deal. Going up."

"I gotta get outta here." Carl looked over the side of the basket. They weren't so high up that he couldn't jump. He slung one leg over the side, but Steve grabbed his arm.

"Carl, don't do it, you'll snap a kneecap. Besides, I think I've got it figured out. It must be one pull for 'up,' two pulls for 'down.'" He yanked the cord twice. It jammed. Flames roared high overhead. The whooshing sound went on and on. The basket rose up.

"It's stuck!" Steve cried out over the noise.

The basket rose higher and higher. High above the wooden platform. High above the roof of the shack. Carl felt the bottom of his stomach drop out and he broke into a sweat. His knees trembled. So long, precious earth!

Higher and higher they rose into the air. Far down below in the field, Jimmy came tearing out of the shack staring up at them. He was waving his arms and jumping up and down, shouting. Was he shouting instructions for how they could bring the balloon back down? If he was, it was impossible to make them out.

"Steve!" Carl cried as they rose up, up, and away above the treetops. "If I ever get down from here alive, I'm gonna kill you for this!"

Eleven

CARL SAT in the bottom of the swaying basket with his eyes sealed shut and his fists clenched. Steve tapped him on the knee, making him nearly jump out of his skin.

"You might as well stand up and enjoy the view," Steve said.

Carl shook his head firmly.

"Look, you're my primo buddy, and I wouldn't see you suffer for the world," Steve began. "But—"

"Then get me down from here." Carl bit off each word.

"In time...in time.... But meanwhile, you might as well take advantage of the situation to work at mastering your fears."

"No," Carl said flatly.

Steve tried again. "Remember last spring when you coached me for that boxing match with Fuffner at Silver's Gym?"

"What's that got to do with anything?" Carl growled.

"It's got to do with fear," Steve said. "You think I wasn't just as scared then as you are now? Why, I knew perfectly well that Fuffner could have killed me. Or, if not killed me, at least destroyed my good looks and maimed me for life."

"So?"

"So the point is, even though I was scared out of my wits, I stepped up to my fears and stared them down. I *made* myself be the Lean, Mean Urkel Machine, even though I felt like Sniveling Steve on the inside. The time has come for you, Carl Winslow, to transform yourself into the Lean, Mean Winslow Machine."

What Steve was saying had the uncomfortable ring of truth. If Carl didn't overcome his fears, he might lose his badge. And if he lost his badge, he'd lose his self-respect. And if he lost that, he risked losing everything.

"Say it," Steve commanded. "Just say it to yourself. 'I'm a Lean, Mean Winslow Machine.'" Steve stood up. "Think of me as your coach, Carl. Just like you coached me through that fight, I'll coach you through this. Remember, Big Fella, I'm in your corner."

Carl nodded his head. 'I'm a Lean, Mean Winslow Machine," he said to himself a few times. He wasn't sure if he believed it or not.

He looked up at Steve, who was offering him his hand. Steve at least looked like *he* believed it. Carl took Steve's hand and stood up, fighting for balance in the swaying basket. He shut his eyes tight, not really wanting to look down. He didn't want to feel those swirly-swirlies welling up in him—again.

"Open your eyes, Carl. Believe me, this view will take your breath away," he heard Steve whisper in his ear.

"That's exactly what I'm afraid of," Carl said. Nevertheless, he opened his eyes. Very slowly, he looked down.

The suburbs of Chicago stretched out beneath him. Roofs and lawns formed a pretty patchwork quilt. Cars swarmed everywhere like tiny multi-colored ants.

Ants! Carl smiled dizzily. Then he dived back into the basket to save himself from fainting. Meanwhile, they continued to sail on into the wild blue yonder—now over the great city of Chicago.

"Okay," Steve said, "you're doing fine. I want you to stand up and look down again. Only this time, a little longer."

Carl steeled himself. He stood up. Gripping the rim of the basket, he looked down.

Funny, the Sears Tower actually looked small from up here.

"Very good, Carl." Steve's voice was soothing. "You're making some real progress here."

"Yeah," Carl agreed, seconds before he fainted.

When he came to, he pulled himself up to stand again. Was that a pigeon or an eagle that was flying past them?

"Can you get us down, Steve? Can you?" Carl pleaded.

"Relax, Carl. When the air inside the balloon cools, we'll begin to float down. Now, we don't know where or when but those are the imponderables that make life interesting."

Carl pointed over to where Lake Michigan stretched out endlessly to the north, as vast as an ocean. Would they drift out over there and plunge to a watery death?

"Don't worry," Steve said, following Carl's glance. "The prevailing winds are such that we probably won't go in that direction."

Carl sagged with relief. Then he heard a dull roar just over his left shoulder. "What's that noise?"

"Why, it's an airplane, a 747, Carl. And it appears to be heading right at us."

Carl ducked and uselessly covered his head. "How close is it gonna come to us?"

Steve squinted. "Let me put it this way. They're serving Tomato Surprise for lunch."

As the massive 747 buzzed them, the basket swung wildly in the wake of its jet stream. Carl held on tight. When he felt fairly balanced, he looked over to check on Steve.

"Steve!" Carl screamed. Where was he? One minute he had been standing across from Carl. The next minute he was gone!

Twelve

"STEVE! STEVE!"

In a panic, Carl lunged to look over the side of the basket. Where had the kid gone? He couldn't have just disappeared into thin air. Unless...Carl swallowed hard. Unless, in the turbulence of the jet's passing, Steve had been thrown overboard? *No*, Carl told himself, *please let Steve be okay!*

Mentally, Carl took back every nasty thing he had ever thought of or said to the guy. And how was he going to break it to Dr. and Mrs. Urkel? But what did he have to worry about? Without Steve along for the ride, he'd never get down alive.

Suddenly, it seemed awfully lonely up there, with nothing but the wind for company.

Then he heard a high, squeaky sound. It sounded

like a cross between a fire alarm and a sick calf.

"Carl! Carl!"

Carl stepped to the other side of the basket and leaned out. Trailing about twenty feet behind the basket, hanging on by a single slender rope, was Steve. His long legs dangled in thin air. His feet in saddle shoes scrambled madly for a foothold which wasn't there.

Carl got hold of the rope. "Hang on, Steve... hang on!"

Setting aside his own fears, Carl began to haul in the rope with all his might. Every pull of the rope brought Steve another foot closer to the basket and to safety. Finally, Steve was close enough for Carl to reach out and grab hold of his arm.

He reached out but missed by a few inches. Not quite close enough. Carl climbed up onto a coil of rope which brought him that extra few inches closer to Steve. Also closer to falling overboard himself. But what did it matter? A life was at stake here.

Carl reached out his hand toward Steve.

Bingo! He managed to get hold of Steve's sweater. He pulled, but the sweater began slipping off! Steve screamed. Carl lunged even farther out of the basket to get a better hold beneath Steve's arm. Carl's weight tilted the basket, nearly dumping him out.

For a split second, both Steve and Carl hung out in space, high over Greater Chicago. Then, with a mighty heave, Carl brought them both back inside the basket. They lay in the bottom of the basket, panting. Steve clung to Carl as if his life still depended upon it.

"You okay?" Carl asked breathlessly.

Steve nodded. Finally, he found his voice. The voice Carl had been so sure, only moments ago, he would never hear again.

Snort. Snort. Laugh. Laugh. "I think so, Carl. Whew, I just stared Ol' Man Death right in the face. Lemme tell you, he's one ugly dude."

They lay there awhile longer, pulling themselves together. Then Steve sat up. "Hey, Carl, do you realize what you just did?"

Carl shrugged wearily.

"You just saved my life."

Carl nodded.

"And, just as important, you forgot about your fear of heights. You did what you had to do without even thinking about it. In that instant, you truly were transformed from Carl the Catwalk Coward to the Lean, Mean Winslow Machine."

It slowly dawned on Carl that Steve was right. He, Carl Winslow, had played acrobat on the rim of a basket sailing thousands of feet up in the air. No sweat. No tears. No swirly-swirlies.

Steve put a hand on Carl's shoulder. "I now pronounce you cured."

Just to be sure, Carl rose to his feet again. He looked out over the rim of the basket. It was pretty far down, all right. But he saw the view clearly and steadily. In fact, he almost appreciated it. Chicago looked pretty good from this angle.

"I think your job worries are over, Big Guy," Steve said. "In the air and on the ground, you're still a cop's cop. A top cop. A no-holds-barred nonstop cop. And, if you ask me, you're the best cop in the world."

Thirteen

CARL SAVORED the last Mississippi mud cookie and smiled warmly at the memory.

"I'll never forget it. After I saved his scrawny neck, Steve piloted that baby like he was born in a balloon. Come to think of it, maybe he was."

Just then, the "pilot" himself walked in the front door—without knocking as usual. He joined right in the conversation without missing a beat.

"You see, once I understood the physics of it, Carl, it was nothing. Living with my father, you learn a lot about hot air."

Mother Winslow giggled.

Rachel cleared her throat loudly.

"Thank you for sharing that with us," Harriette said.

"What brings you back?" Laura wanted to know.

Steve looked at Laura. Then he looked at Rachel's earrings lying on the coffee table. It looked as if she had long since given up trying to put them on.

"I brought you a present, my dear," he said.

Laura looked uneasy. "What?" she asked.

He handed her a small velvet-covered box. It looked very old.

She looked at the box, then at him.

"What is it?"

"Open it," he urged her.

Laura shrugged and opened the box. She gasped.

Nestled in the box's pearl-gray velvet lining was a pair of earrings.

Laura took them out and held them up to the light.

The women crowded in to get a closer look. They were pearls. Genuine pearls. In a simple but elegant gold setting. Laura's jaw dropped.

"But these are priceless, Steve!" Laura said. "Aren't they?"

"Correctaroonie," Steve said. "They were my

grandmother Urkel's. She left them to me...to give to some deserving young lady, someday. I think that day has come."

"But...but..." Laura stammered.

"They're a lot more delicate than those cast-iron chandeliers you were contemplating earlier. I confess I couldn't stand the thought of those monstrosities stretching your lovely lobes."

"So you're giving me these genuine pearls?" Laura shook her head and stared at the earrings. Then at Steve. He never ceased to amaze her. He was certainly full of surprises.

"Thank you, Steve," she said gently. In that instant, she made up her mind about what had to be done.

"Sweets to the sweet, I always say, my precious pearl. Well..." He shifted awkwardly from foot to foot. "I guess I'll be moseying along. Wear them in health...on your date with Greg tonight."

"What date with Greg?" Laura said.

Halfway to the door, Steve froze. He turned. "You mean, you don't have a date after all?"

"You don't expect me to wait around the house on the slim chance he'll finish studying in time to spare me a few moments of his precious time, do you?"

Laura went over to the mirror and put on her new earrings. They fitted as if they had been made for her. She turned around and modeled them, smiling.

The women oohed and aahed. Even Carl was impressed.

"Well, Steve..." Laura said. "Ready for our date?"

Steve took a quick look behind him to see if some other Steve were the lucky man.

"Steve," Carl said, "I'm pretty sure she means you. Why don't you just grin and enjoy it."

Steve shrugged. Then he held out a gallant arm to Laura.

"For you, my sweet, I will brave the most horrendous horror movie."

"Sure you won't be afraid?" she teased him.

"Me? The Lean, Mean Urkel Machine? Afraid of a few grisly, not even halfway convincing special effects? Surely, you jest."

And with a snort, snort, and a laugh, he escorted his date out into the evening.